For Lucy ❦ M. D.

For Lucy and Dee, I grew ❦ C. C.

Text copyright © 2003 by Malachy Doyle
Illustrations copyright © 2003 by Carll Cneut

First U.S. edition 2003

Library of Congress Cataloging-in-Publication Data

Doyle, Malachy.
Antonio on the other side of the world, getting smaller / Malachy Doyle;
illustrated by Carll Cneut. — 1st U.S. ed.
p.   cm.
Summary: Antonio has fun visiting his grandmother but misses his mother
so much that he starts to shrink, and as he travels back to the other side of
the world by ship, train, and horse, he gets smaller and smaller.
ISBN 0-7636-2173-0
[1. Size — Fiction. 2. Travel — Fiction. 3. Mother and child — Fiction.
4. Grandmothers — Fiction.] I. Cneut, Carll, ill. II. Title.
PZ7.D775 An 2003
[E] — dc21   2002035127

10 9 8 7 6 5 4 3 2 1

Printed in China

This book was typeset in Mrs. Eaves.
The illustrations were done in acrylic.

Candlewick Press
2067 Massachusetts Avenue
Cambridge, Massachusetts 02140

visit us at www.candlewick.com

Antonio

on the Other Side
of the World, Getting Smaller

illustrated by

MALACHY DOYLE ◊ CARLL CNEUT

CANDLEWICK PRESS
CAMBRIDGE, MASSACHUSETTS

Antonio went to visit his wonderful gran on a tiny island on the other side of the world.

They had a whale of a time, paddling around in Granny's boat and tossing jam sandwiches to the snippy-snappy sea monsters.

But after a week and a whole heap of fun,
Antonio couldn't reach the
oars anymore.

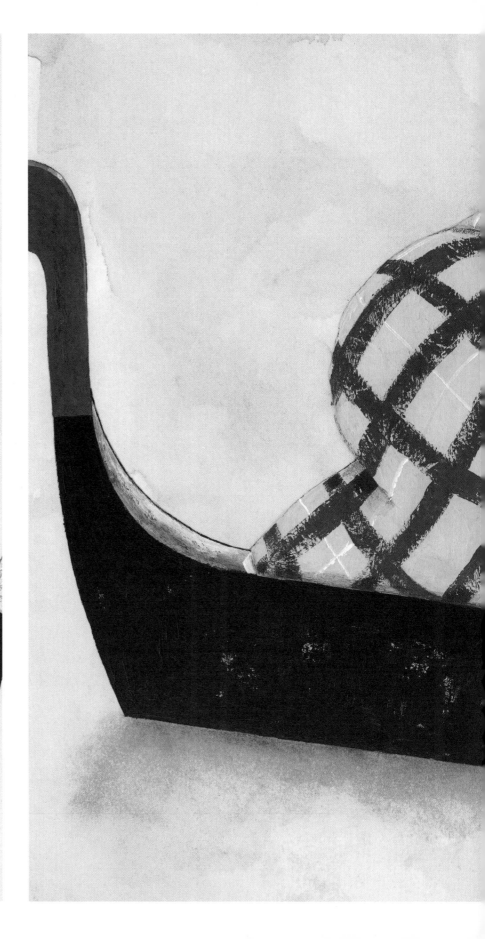

And after another week
and another heap of fun,
he couldn't even see over
the side of the boat.

"I love having you here, Antonio," said Gran.

"But you're only half the size you were when you came.

You miss your mom—that's the problem.

You miss your mom, and it's time to go home."

So his granny made him another big bag of jam sandwiches,

kissed the top of his sweet little head, and sent him on his way.

Antonio got a job on a ship,

sailing for home.

"You're a little small for a cabin boy,"

said the old captain.

"But I suppose you'll do."

It was hard work

and rough seas, but

"I'm on the way home!"

sang Antonio happily.

"For I want to be home with my mother!"

Little Antonio reached dry land at last,

but by now he was smaller still.

A whole heap smaller.

"You're too little for an engine boy,"

said the train driver. "But I'll see

if I can find you a job."

So Antonio rode up front

to watch out for sheep on the tracks.

"I'm on the way home!" he cried to the sheep.

"I'm on the way home to my mother!"

And he blasted a blast on

the whistle. *Wheeee!*

When Antonio got off the train, he spotted a cowboy,

climbing down from a hard day in the saddle.

"Do you think I could have a ride on your horse, sir?"

said little Antonio. *"For I'm on the way home,"*

he sang, with a smile. *"I'm on the way home to my mother."*

"You're a little small for a cowboy,"

said the man, peering down at him.

"But you can borrow my horse if you'd like.

She's much too lively for me."

So up Antonio jumped
and off he galloped.

"Yes, I'm on the way home!"

he cried as he rode.

"I'm on the way home to my mother!"

And he hung on tightly, did the brave Antonio,

till he'd ridden the range and tamed the wild horse, too . . .

though by now he was only a slip of a thing,

what with being away from home so long.

Finally, finally, Antonio got to his house,
but he was so tiny that his mother
didn't notice him.

"Hi, Mom!" he squeaked, but she couldn't
even see him, and she hardly even heard him.
"What's that?" she said, looking all around.
"Is it a mouse?"

"It's me, your son!" cried Antonio, pulling on her skirt.

"Who's there?" said his mother.

"Is it an imp?"

Little Antonio jumped up on the table,
right in front of her eyes, and yelled,
"It's me, Antonio, home at last!"

Well, wasn't she amazed at
the sight of her son—home
from afar, but oh, so small!
She hugged him and kissed him,
put him on her knee and said,
"It's great to have you back, dear,
but you could do with
some fattening up."

So she fed him bread and she
fed him milk, she fed him meat
and she fed him carrots,
she fed him cake and she
fed him porridge,
till he grew,
and he grew
and he grew.

In time Antonio was so tall that he

could sit on his roof, shout,

"IT'S GOOD TO BE HOME!"

and wave to his wonderful gran on the

other side of the world.

And his granny waved back.